PUFFIN BOOKS

OVER THE MOON AND FAR AWAY

Ben and his friends don't know what to make of the new girl, Zillah, when she joins their class on the first day of term. She doesn't wear a school uniform, she's never heard of wheelbarrow races, and she doesn't even know what chocolate tastes like. But there are other things she does know about – like the fearful curse on the lake, for instance – and she seems able to make things happen, just by thinking about them.

But does Zillah really possess special powers? Why does she always wear that strange flashing prism round her neck? And what is her connection with the mysterious, shawled old woman with the brightly coloured headscarf?

Zillah is a mystery, wherever she comes from, but life is nothing if not eventful when she's around. You could almost believe that she does indeed come from 'over the moon and far away'.

Margaret Nash was born in Yorkshire. She was educated at Bradford Grammar School, and then qualified as a Chartered Librarian. She worked in various libraries, before becoming a secretary in a local village school. She is married with two children.

Other books by Margaret Nash

LOLLIPOP DAYS
RAT SATURDAY

MARGARET NASH

Over the Moon and Far Away

ILLUSTRATED BY KEITH BRUMPTON

PUFFIN BOOKS

PUFFIN BOOKS

Published by the Penguin Group
27 Wrights Lane, London W8 5TZ, England
Viking Penguin Inc., 40 West 23rd Street, New York, New York 10010, USA
Penguin Books Australia Ltd, Ringwood, Victoria, Australia
Penguin Books Canada Ltd, 2801 John Street, Markham, Ontario, Canada L3R 1B4
Penguin Books (NZ) Ltd, 182–190 Wairau Road, Auckland 10, New Zealand

Penguin Books Ltd, Registered Offices: Harmondsworth, Middlesex, England

First published by Viking Kestrel 1989
Published in Puffin Books 1990
10 9 8 7 6 5 4 3 2 1

Text copyright © Margaret Nash, 1989
Illustrations copyright © Keith Brumpton, 1989
All rights reserved

Printed and bound in Great Britain by
Cox & Wyman Ltd, Reading
Set in Palatino

Chapter 1

It all began on the first day of the
summer term, just after Miss Bell had
called the register. Ben glanced up as
the door slowly opened and a new girl
walked in. She was tall and bony and
awkward-looking, like a spiky twig.
There was not even a hint of school-
grey about her. She wore odd socks,

and around her neck hung a glass prism. It sparkled the colours of her stripy jumper around the classroom.

Miss Bell's biro fell from her fingers and she shuffled some papers on her desk.

"Now let me see. You must be . . ."

"Zillah," said the girl, smiling a little.

"Ah, yes, Zillah. Our new girl, is that right?"

"Yes, I'm a traveller," said the new girl.

Some children began chattering. Miss Bell stood up and they stopped.

"Do you think you will be with us long, Zillah?" The girl smiled and said probably not, then went to the back of the classroom and sat in the empty seat next to Steven. Ben sighed. He'd been sitting there until Miss Bell had

moved him for talking. She was
annoying like that, was Miss Bell. She
was always separating people for
talking.

Miss Bell sat back comfortably and
began the term in her usual way.
"Now, Class Three, who has
something interesting to tell us about
the holidays?"

Ben stared out of the window at his
special tree on the distant hillside. It
shone like gold in the blue sky. He

remembered his mother telling him to concentrate this term. "Less of your dreaming and forgetfulness," she'd said. He switched back to the talking.

"Don't tell tarrydiddles, Lucy," Miss Bell was saying.

"You mean lies, Miss," said Conrad Jones in his swanky voice. Miss Bell ignored him.

"I did. I did go to the pond alone at night," said Lucy. Surely she wouldn't go there at night, not timid little Lucy Clements. Ben looked back at the tree. He'd never go near that evil place at night, not if someone gave him the moon. He thought of its green, sour water and shiny scum swirling in ghostly evening mist and shuddered. How could she? They all knew not to go near the village pond after what had happened there.

8

"Are you sure you didn't dream it, Lucy?" said Miss Bell.

Lucy's cheeks suddenly became very red. She cupped her hand over her mouth for a second then said quietly, "But . . . but it was very real, Miss Bell and it . . . it didn't seem frightening any more. I'm sure . . ." She stopped and scratched her head.

"Dreams can be very realistic, dear," said Miss Bell, "but we're not talking about dreams at the moment, Lucy." She went on to ask Steven what he'd done.

At lunchtime Jonathan Turvey and Conrad Jones started on Lucy. "Lucy Lucy Locket has dreams in her pocket." Suddenly a long shadow crept in front of them all, and behind it stood the new girl. She laid a gentle hand on Lucy's shoulder.

"I don't think you were silly," she said. "There's a lot more to dreams than people think."

"Nobody cares what you think, gypsy girl," said Conrad. "You're new."

"No, I'm not. In fact, I'm very, very old and I'm not a gypsy girl. I'm a traveller." Before Conrad could say any more the dinner bell rang and everyone rushed in to get a seat at the back, out of the dinner ladies' way.

Ben found himself next to Zillah. When the gravy came round she poured some into her water glass, and when the sausages arrived she picked one up as though it were a banana and started peeling its skin.

"What a good idea," said Andrew Stone, who liked trying anything silly. He copied. So did Alison. So did

Steven. So did Ben, except his sausage broke and landed in his tumbler. That sent them all crazy with laughter. He could see Miss Bell forcing her fat hips through the narrow aisles in an effort to see what they were laughing at.

"Quick!" he said and they all

poured gravy back on to their plates
and put down the sausages. Zillah
picked up her knife and fork.

"Where I come from we don't have
these," she said, "but they look fun."
She laughed, a short curly sort of
laugh.

"It's a roly-poly pudding for afters,"
said Steven. "We usually roll it round
the playground a couple of times
before we eat it." Zillah looked as
though she might believe him.

"Take no notice of him," said Ben.
"He's bonkers. Him and Andrew
Stone are both bonkers. Miss Bell's

12

always on at them."

"What is a bonker?" asked Zillah. Alison laughed out loud and Ben saw Miss Bell look at them again.

"Quiet," he said. "We don't want old Ring-a-ding back. She goes bonkers too sometimes."

As they filed out of the dining-room Steven grabbed him. "Hey, do you think Zillah really is a gypsy? I mean she's strange, sort of odd but fun. She's not like a gypsy, yet she's not like us either, and if she's not a gypsy, then who is she and where is she from?"

"Don't know," said Ben, "but I expect we'll find out."

"Fancy not knowing what 'bonkers' means," said Andrew. "Did you tell her?"

"No," said Ben.

Chapter 2

The evening sunlight streamed on to the table like a laser beam while Ben was eating tea. It was blooming annoying having to dodge out of its way all the time, especially as his mother was going on about him dreaming again and forgetting to call at the shop. Suddenly he remembered something else. He'd forgotten to post Dad's letters on his way to school. He didn't feel like tea any more. He pushed the chair from the table and stood up.

"Going to take Bimbo for a walk for old Mrs Turner," he said, hurriedly brushing cake crumbs off his mouth and went towards the door. "See you, Mum."

He posted the letters at the corner just by Mrs Turner's, then opened the gate. Mrs Turner heaved herself out of a chair where she'd been sitting in a patch of early-evening sunlight and limped towards him, clutching her swollen knee. Bimbo rushed up to him.

"Ee, but 'e does love you, Ben," she said. The dog put his head on one side, letting his brown, patchy ear droop over his white face. He made small woofling noises. Ben wished he could do something as appealing for his mother or Miss Bell when they went on about him forgetting things.

Mrs Turner steered herself round and fetched the dog's lead. Ben fixed it, then ran off with Bimbo to the common.

On a tree stump, near the pond, sat Zillah. She had her head in her hands and was staring into the murky water.

Ben shouted across to her. She jumped up and came running towards them. Bimbo stopped his snuffling into a paper bag he'd found and looked up. His fur stood up like bristles on a brush, and he took a few steps backwards and howled.

"Don't be silly, Bimbo," said Ben. The dog stopped howling but gave a low, rumbling growl. His ears went back like triangular flags and his eyes took on a wild glint.

"I've never seen him like this before," said Ben. Zillah shuffled uneasily.

"He knows I'm not from these parts. He'll be all right in a moment, you'll see." She bent down in front of the lead. Ben shortened it in case the new wild Bimbo should snap her nose off. But Zillah stared hard at the dog, and as she did so his eyes lost their wild look. He wagged his stumpy tail and ran round her in circles. It was as though she magicked him friendly.

"He's ripping," said Zillah,

"What do you mean 'ripping'?" said Ben.

"Oh, isn't that what you say?" said Zillah.

"No," said Ben. "Ripping is tearing. We rip up paper. We say 'brill'."

"Oh," said Zillah in a disappointed voice. "Well, brill then. Where I come from all animals roam free. We don't have them on strings."

"Whereabouts *do* you come from?" asked Ben.

"Oh, from over the moon and far away," laughed Zillah.

"Seriously," said Ben. "Are you from France or somewhere like that?"

"No. Further away."

"Australia?"

"No. Much, much further," said Zillah, and her eyes had a misty distant look about them. At that moment Steven and the others appeared, carrying cricket gear.

Once Zillah got the hang of the game she streaked up and down the pitch on her long legs, scoring runs. Conrad couldn't get her out. In the end he gave up and wore a scowl for the rest of the evening.

"It's a ripp . . . I mean fab game," said Zillah as they all flopped down to rest. "I wonder if I could hit the ball into outer space? Perhaps if I ate some energy dust . . ."

"'Course you could," interrupted Andrew, stretching his arms upwards as if reaching for the sky. "I do it often!"

"Oh, yes," said Steven. "You just whack it into the copse and lose the blooming ball, you do. Or worse still, into the pond where we daren't get it out."

"Why are you all so frightened of

the pond?" said Zillah. "And why daren't you get the ball out?"

No one said anything. Ben shrugged. A stranger might not believe them. You needed to live in Middle Hill to know the evils of the pond.

"I'm hot and thirsty," said Andrew, raking a hand through his mass of brown curls.

"Hold on – I'll get the ice-cream man here," said Zillah.

Ben sat up and looked. "But he's right up the road. You need binoculars to see him."

"That's no problem," said Zillah. "Not with telepathy." She put her head in her hands and sat absolutely still like a zombie.

"Whatever are you doing?" asked Conrad.

She pushed strands of long fair hair off her face. "Oh, don't you do telepathy here on Earth? You should. It's the science of the future is telepathy."

"Telepathy! You're cracked!" said Conrad. Even Steven looked stunned and usually nothing amazed him.

Ben watched Lucy pleating bits of her skirt. She always did that when she was nervous. Ben remembered his own attempts at telepathy. "You have to concentrate your thoughts into someone else's mind," he said. "I once tried it on you, Alison, when it was cheese pie for dinner. I tried to make you leave yours so I could have it, but you gobbled it all up and asked for seconds. By the time I'd finished my telepathy there was none left."

"Can you do it because you're a gypsy?" asked Lucy quietly. Lucy was small but she looked even smaller sitting between Alison and Zillah.

Zillah seemed to search the distance with her dark eyes. "I've told you: I'm not a gypsy, I'm a traveller. Gypsies travel the world. I travel much further."

"Go on," said Conrad, "you're making it up. You reckon you're so clever and yet you couldn't do your sums this afternoon. But then gypsies don't get much schooling. We're always miles ahead of them."

"Not always," said Lucy. "My dad

23

once knew a gypsy who could add up any number of figures quickly. He did it all in his head too."

Conrad scowled even more. He was the best in the class at sums and knew it.

Zillah stood up and turned to face him. She stood with her hands on her narrow hips and pushed her chin forward. "Well, you're wrong, Conrad. I'm not behind you. I'm ahead of you, and not just miles ahead – light years ahead, so there. From

over the moon and beyond your
furthest star, that's where I'm from."
She suddenly calmed down.
"Anyway I don't care if you don't
believe me. Look, here comes the
ice-cream man. I'm off." She shot
across the common to where the
blue-and-white van was just pulling to
a halt.

"Gosh, it must have worked," said
Alison.

"She's having us on," said Andrew.
"She must be."

"I don't know," said Lucy, skimming her foot across the grass. "She's different."

"You're daft," said Conrad. "I bet you believe the moon's made of green cheese."

"Let's follow her," said Andrew. "Come on." But Zillah was no longer at the ice-cream van. They looked round the common and searched the village, but Zillah was nowhere to be seen.

"Well, I intend to find out if she's a gypsy or not," said Conrad, "and I know how. It's easy."

Chapter 3

Steven was in the middle of a knot of excited pupils when Ben arrived in the playground next morning. He grabbed Ben's arm and drew him into the circle.

"We're all meeting at six o'clock this evening and going to the gypsy site to see if Zillah lives there. If she is a gypsy, she will do. It's the only gypsy site around for miles. Oh, shhh. She's coming."

Zillah was walking towards them, her glass prism glinting in the sun. As she arrived the sun suddenly jerked behind a cloud and it started raining. Everyone except Zillah ran towards the door. Ben looked up through the silver rain. He saw the faint arc of a rainbow. Zillah looked at it too. She shielded her eyes.

"The colours are so beautiful, Ben. They remind me of my home, my real home." Ben wasn't sure, but he thought her eyes looked damp. Surely she wasn't crying. He agreed with Lucy. He wouldn't bet on her being a gypsy girl at all. They went slowly indoors.

Ben couldn't settle to lessons. Miss Bell was planning a ramble for the

next day, but he only half listened.
She asked him twice if he was
dreaming. He started wondering if his
Auntie Bessie would give him 50p
when she came at the weekend. She
sometimes did. He got a sudden
prickly feeling down his spine, like an
itch that crawled. He fidgeted.
Everyone else was working. Everyone
except Zillah. She was smiling at him
and nodding her head. When she held
up 50p Ben could hardly believe it. His
prickles multiplied and he stopped
listening to Miss Bell altogether.

The afternoon went more quickly. They did painting, and Mr Spriggott, the headteacher, came into the room. Mr Spriggott hardly ever interrupted classes, especially in the afternoons. Steven said he did the newspaper crossword puzzle in his office in an afternoon, but Ben's dad said that was silly talk. Mr Spriggott beamed at Miss Bell, then wandered round the classroom to see what they were doing. He stopped by Zillah's desk, then whistled through his teeth.

"My word!" he exclaimed. "Have you seen this, Miss Bell?"

Miss Bell bustled over, poking wisps of greying hair into her neat bun. She stared hard at the painting, then took her glasses off and leaned closer. Class Three watched. At last she held it up for them all to see.

Zillah had drawn a scene as though it were inside a bowl. The trees curved inwards at the tops, and down the centre was a winding path. But the most remarkable thing about the picture was the colour. Blues blended smoothly into greens and yellows. The sky was a misty rose-pink with shades of orange. In among the grass and trees were lots of tiny animals, each one perfectly drawn.

"Where is this place, Zillah?"

"It's my garden."

Miss Bell stood back and touched her hair again, as if to check that it was still there.

Mr Spriggott clapped his hands in front of him. "Oh, such talent, such imagination!" he said. "It would look lovely in the hall. I've never seen such work, have you, Miss Bell?" He didn't give Miss Bell time to answer before he clapped his hands again, then walked slowly to the front of the class. His shoes squeaked all the way to the door, and he left rubbing his hands and repeating the word "amazing" as though he'd only just discovered the word.

After that Miss Bell let them clear away, and they were all lined up for home even before the bell went. Ben tried to find Zillah, but as usual she'd gone. It seemed as though one second she was there and the next second she wasn't.

"Don't forget, six o'clock at the pillar box," said Andrew. "See you."

At ten minutes to six there came a growling and barking through the letter box. It was Steven. Steven always did something daft when he called. He was standing there, pawing the air and panting when Ben opened the door.

"Thought it was Bimbo, you wally," said Ben. "Come on."

"Don't be too long," called his mother. "Remember: you promised Dad you'd help strip the wallpaper off your bedroom wall tonight."

The others were already at the pillar box, all except Jonathan Turvey. He'd had to go to bed with stomach ache. Ben was glad. He was a troublemaker was Jonathan Turvey. Alison was wearing pink-and-white striped trousers. She looked like a stick of rock, but she thought herself dead fashionable.

The village of Middle Hill was only small. Once they'd passed the common the houses were few and far between, and very posh. Then there

34

was a long stretch of road with no footpath until they turned left into what was called the Lane. It was a steep uphill climb.

"Nearly there," puffed Andrew. "It's just round the next corner behind those trees." The site was hidden from the road, but once over the stile they were surrounded by caravans. There was washing draped on bushes, a few old cars and piles of scrap metal. A smell of bonfires hung around but

there was no sign of anybody at all. It was a place of silence. Even the birds had stopped singing. They were still walking in single file and Lucy was almost pushing Ben. Conrad was striding away in front. No one talked.

They climbed another stile into a large field and wandered over to an old-fashioned caravan in the corner. It was shut up but the windows were clean and sparkled in the evening sun. Alison walked round it.

"Give us a bunk up on to the wheel," she said.

"Mind your posh white shoes," said Conrad, holding her steady.

"What can you see?" asked Steven.

Alison looked through the window but said nothing. She was like that. She kept things to herself and was annoying with it. She still didn't answer. She jumped down, and turned to Ben. "You look."

Ben peered through, cupping his hands to get a better view.

"In the corner through that doorway," said Alison.

"Cripes!" said Ben.

Conrad was clawing at his back. "Come on, let me."

"Shhh," said Ben. "There's someone here." Sitting slumped in a chair, muffled up in a black shawl, was a woman. A brightly coloured head square had slipped partly over

37

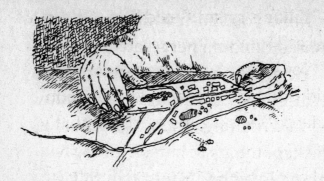

her face. She looked dead. But
suddenly she snorted and shook. Ben
jumped down quickly but not before
he'd seen something else. On a low
table next to the woman were a map
and a twig shaped like the letter "Y".
Ben knew what that was. It was a
water-divining twig. His Uncle Bob
said you could hold them and they'd
swing when water was near. But more
interesting than that was what was
peeping out from under the map. It
was a glass prism on a chain. He
jumped down.

38

"Zillah's prism," said Ben. "It's in there."

"Told you it was a load of bunkum," said Conrad. "'From over the moon' indeed. She's a gypsy girl and that's that."

They ran back through the site. From somewhere far away two rifle shots sounded. Ben thought his heart would jump out of his mouth, but they just kept on running and didn't stop till they were half way down the Lane.

"I suppose she must be a gypsy after all," gasped Alison.

"Funny her telling us about light years and all that," said Andrew. "She doesn't seem the sort of girl to lie."

"Cor," said Steven as they collapsed on the common. "I never want to go there again, whether she's from outer space or under the sea."

The first thing Ben saw when he felt rested enough to sit upright was Zillah. She was sitting calmly against the horrible pond, watching them. He gave a long groan and sank back to the ground. When he looked again she had gone.

Chapter 4

"Did you see her?" he said.

"See who?" Conrad flapped his Superman tee-shirt to let in air.

"Zillah."

"No."

"But she was over there," said Ben. Conrad stared at the empty tree stump.

"You're going bonkers, Ben. You'll be seeing space ships next."

"There she is! Look!" said Andrew suddenly jumping to his feet. "Over there by the pond." Sure enough, Zillah was now sitting on the low willow-tree branch which overhung the pond.

"You wait, gypsy girl," said Conrad. "We'll sort this out once and for all." But Zillah came bounding up, so pleased to see them that no one, not even Conrad, said anything.

"What's this ramble thing tomorrow?" she said, settling herself down beside Alison. "I've never heard of one. Is it a party?"

"No, it's a walk," said Alison.

"But it's called a ramble because Miss Bell rambles on and on about

village history during it," said
Andrew. "Boring, boring."

Zillah laughed. "I'd rather have a
party. Can't we turn it into one?"

"You're joking."

"What's joking?"

"You know," said Steven, "don't
you?"

Zillah looked across the common.
"Tell me about this pond you're all so
scared of. You know, the one Lucy
dreamed about. Is that boring, boring
too?"

They all went silent. Alison dug the toe of her shoe into the ground, then spent the next few minutes spitting and rubbing out the grass stain.

"We don't go near the pond," said Ben. "Not since Tommy Harris you-know-what." He looked at Steven.

"What?" said Zillah. "Since Tommy Harris did what?"

"He drowned, that's what," said Steven.

"And was he joking?"

"'Course not," said Steven. "Don't be silly. He died."

"And he wasn't the only one," said Andrew. "Some peculiar things have happened near that pond since some old witch put a curse on it years and years ago. Dogs and cats have sunk without trace."

"My Grandad's school friend went through the ice one winter," said Andrew. "He died. It's a horrid pond."

"You see, it used to be a witches' ducking pond," said Alison. She held up the shoe for inspection. "And one day an old lady, who everyone said was a witch, put a curse on it, so the story goes."

"Well, take the curse off," said Zillah. "The pond would look lovely cleaned up with swimming animals in it."

"Don't be stupid, gypsy girl," said Conrad. "How can we take the curse off? By the way, you *are* a gypsy girl, aren't you? We saw that prism thing of yours in a gypsy trailer on the site up the Lane."

Zillah put her hand down the neck

of her jumper and brought out the prism. She lifted it up and a ray of evening sun caught it and shone a blue diamond right into Conrad's left eye. "You know a lot of things," she said, "but they are not always right."

"Well, do you live there, or don't you?" asked Steven. "Because there was an old lady there too, muffled up in a shawl on an evening like this. It's a wonder she didn't suffocate."

"We've only been sitting in there for a while," said Zillah. "It's hot where we come from. We've got two suns, and she feels the cold here. She only just made the journey. She's very, very old."

"Well, why did she come?" asked Alison.

"To do what had to be done," said Zillah.

"What do you mean?" said Conrad. "Go on, tell us."

But Zillah shook her head.

"Well, how can we believe you then?" said Andrew.

Zillah took something out of her pocket. It was rubbery, like a cactus leaf, but square and purple. "These leaves hold water for hundreds of years," she said, "even when they come off from the plant. You don't have leaves like this here. It will not die in your lifetime."

Ben took it and the others looked. It had a dusty surface and shimmered slightly, but it was as fresh as if it had just come off a plant. He held it up to the light, but Zillah reached up and took it back.

"Anyway, I'm enjoying your Earth,

but what I didn't realize was that Earth people have almost no space powers, like telepathy. You all think I'm pretending. It's a pity, but it doesn't matter. I'll stay a while longer. Now, what about uncursing this pond? I'm sure I can do that. You can all help. It will be fun."

Ben thought he saw a sort of bronze glow outlining her body. It reminded him of a porridge advert he'd seen on television.

"Yes," said Alison. "Come on, let's have a go. There's safety in numbers."

The sun was just sliding behind the tall trees at the edge of the common, and the pond seemed to get darker and gloomier as they approached it. Ben shuddered. It always smelled dank. Andrew threw a stone in. It landed in the middle of a patch of

yellow scum and hardly disturbed it.
There never seemed to be any
movement in the pond. It was lifeless.

"I know what you mean," said
Zillah. "It has an unhappy feel about
it."

"What we need is a curse-removing
ceremony," said Steven.

"The more ceremony the better,"
said Andrew, throwing his arms
about wildly. You could tell he was
keen.

"Cere-money!" said Zillah. "Can't we use English money?" She took some coins out of her pocket. "Is this enough? Why should it be cere-money?"

"Honestly, space girl," said Andrew.

Alison leaned on Zillah's shoulder and snorted. "Yes, you are funny sometimes!"

Steven pulled them away from the edge. "Don't fall in. It's not uncursed yet."

"Well, let's get on with it," said Andrew. "We'll collect sticks and stones, then chuck them all in and really make the old water move."

"Yes, brill! We'll stir it all up and splash it everywhere and disturb any evil spirits. We'll show it we're not afraid," said Ben.

"And when we've finished we'll see about having it tidied up and turned into an animal swimming pond," said Zillah.

"You mean a duck pond – quack, quack," said Andrew, flapping his arms and bounding around the pond.

"Yes, quack, quack," said Zillah. "I'm going to fly up into that willow tree."

Ben didn't see her fly, but she was back on the overhanging branch in the blinking of an eye.

They collected sticks and stones. Alison unearthed an old shoe in a paper bag, and Ben found a white bone which he was sure he'd seen Bimbo with once. One by one they hurled things in, getting faster and more and more wild. The water splashed over the edges. It leaped high in the air. It sent ripples and circles zooming over the pond until they collided and splattered everywhere. Alison shouted threats at the water. Andrew flung a half-rotten log in.

Then suddenly Zillah spoke in a voice louder than any of theirs. She stood tall and proud with her arms outstretched and with perfect balance on the thin branch. On her left hand lay a large, flat, shiny stone. "GO, CURSE, FOR EVER!" she yelled and

hurled the stone. As it hit the pond a huge water spout shot upwards so high that it wet her face. She laughed. "That should do it," she said. They all calmed down, and watched the water settle.

"How do we know the curse has gone?" said Conrad. "Someone ought to test it."

No one spoke. Ben looked at the pond. It was as still and miserable as before and looked even gloomier in the fading light.

"I'll test it," said Zillah. "Tomorrow, in this boring, boring ramble thing, I'll test it. I'll jump in. That's what I'll do."

"You can't," said Lucy.

"I can," said Zillah.

"Let her," said Conrad. "We'll see what happens."

Ben suddenly remembered his promise to help his dad with the decorating. He felt pleased to have remembered instead of forgetting. He ran quickly across the common and down the road. Walking slowly towards him was an old lady. She was wearing a black shawl and a brightly coloured head square. As Ben passed her his heart jerked with recognition. Surely it was the woman from the caravan. But when he turned back to look, she'd gone. There was nobody there.

Chapter 5

Ben was late to bed after helping Dad with stripping the paper. It was warm and he couldn't sleep. His model aeroplanes hung heavily from the ceiling, casting shadows on the misty walls. He decided to have a go at concentrating on Zillah. He might have more success with telepathy this time. He leaned back against the bed head and let his breath out slowly. At once he heard a voice. He wondered if he had fallen asleep and was dreaming but, no, it came again.

"Ben, Ben, it's me, Zillah. Can you bring some of your Earth food on the ramble tomorrow?"

Ben was so amazed that his concentration went, but he banged his head on the pillow and said, "Bar of chocolate," three times so that he wouldn't forget. Then he fell asleep. He dreamed of the beautiful picture that Zillah had drawn in class, of a place where there weren't seven colours in the rainbow but twenty, of a place that sent and received radio messages from Planet Earth. After that it got rather complicated, and he knew no more until next morning.

Ben thumped downstairs. Steven was barking through the letter box again. Ben made a quick visit to the biscuit tin for the chocolate, then went to the door.

His mother had opened it and was patting Steven's head with a rolled-up newspaper. Steven always went bright red when Mrs Jarvis entered into the game, but Ben liked it.

"'Bye, Mum," he said, rushing past her, then barked a couple of times at her to let he know she was included.

"Don't forget Mrs Turner's weekly this time," said his mum. "Remember it's Thursday."

"Wuff," he called back.

Mrs Turner was already sitting in her window seat as they passed the corner. She spent ages watching the world go by, did Mrs Turner. They waved, then Ben saw Zillah hurry past the end of the road. "Hang on, I want to ask her something." He left Steven and caught up with Zillah by the pillar box.

"Hey, Zillah, you know that prism of yours that was on the table in your caravan? Well, how could you be wearing it down on the common last night if it was in the caravan?"

"I put it on after I'd been to see Bimbo."

"What, you went to see Bimbo?" Ben didn't feel too pleased. Bimbo was his dog – well, sort of, after Mrs Turner, of course. He frowned, then felt mean and calmed down.

"But we went straight back . . ." began Steven, who had caught up with them. "You couldn't have had time to collect it and get to the common before us."

"Well, I *can* travel at the speed of light."

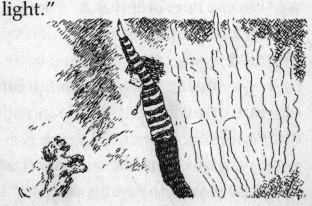

Steven dropped his canvas bag with a thud, right on Ben's big toe.

"Speed of light!"

"Yes. Where I come from, we all can. It takes a lot of effort, mind you, so we don't do it often."

"But you could just keep going in and out like a light bulb," said Ben. "Now you see me, now you don't, sort of thing. You could zot on to school and tell everyone we're on our way. Go on, do it, Zillah. Off you go."

"No, it's hard work and it's boring. What do you say? Oh yes, it's boring, boring. Walking's more fun."

"Walking *fun*!" Ben wrinkled his nose, but Steven jabbed him with his elbow.

"Wheelbarrow walking's fun. Ben and I are good at it." He got down on all fours and made Ben lift up his

knobbly legs with their usual wrinkled socks. Then he wiggled along till he collapsed, dragging Ben down on top of him. They lay there in a heap, laughing.

Zillah jumped up and down. "Let me! Let me!" she squealed. She insisted on wheelbarrow walking all the way to school and made them late. Steven didn't care, but Ben felt stupid arriving at the school gates with her, especially as Steven had draped their satchels round her neck. Miss Bell wasn't amused either.

"You're late," she said. "Now get
with your partners." Steven stood
next to Ben.

"We'll show you three-legged
walking tomorrow," he called. Ben
nudged him to be quiet. But too late.
Miss Bell heard and made Steven go to
the back of the line. Ben had to
partner Lucy, and Lucy wanted to
hold hands like they did in the
Infants', boring, boring.

Miss Bell marched them briskly
across the road to the church. As she
opened the heavy wooden door an
arrow of sunlight shot in front of them

and put diamond-shaped colours on to the cold flagstones. Miss Bell climbed into the pulpit and talked.

She looked silly up there in ordinary clothes. Class Three started shuffling. Word of Zillah's pond-testing had soon spread around the whole class.

At last Miss Bell came down and

they all went out into the warm sunshine. She gave them a few minutes' break to get rid of their fidgeting while she went and sat by the old oak tree.

Ben felt someone tug at him. It was Steven. "Come on. This is it. Let's go over to the pond."

Alison and Andrew were already running across the grass, and he could see Conrad kicking a stone in that direction. They rushed over as quickly as they dared without distracting Miss Bell. The pond looked much the same as usual except that the scum seemed to have divided into two streaks, leaving a dark, desolate stretch in between.

"Zillah's not here yet," said Alison.

"That's great, that is," said Conrad, pushing his long straggly hair off his forehead. "I expect she's over the other side of the moon."

He dabbled his toe in the scum and made patterns. Then he lifted a clump out on his toe.

"Ugh!" said Lucy. "Give over."

"We'd better do some telepathy and get her here," said Alison. "Come on, get started, somebody." But nobody did. Conrad strolled round the edge of the pond, his hands in his pockets. The others just hung around.

Suddenly something creaked sharply above them. Ben looked up. It was Zillah. She was in the tree. No one had seen her arrive. She was springing around pretending to test the tree branches.

"Right, I'm going to jump into the pond." She spread her arms out.

"Just a minute," yelled Ben. "Is

everyone ready?" Conrad had walked half way around the pond. Ben called to him to watch.

"Wait," said Andrew. "Let's do it properly. Let's have a count-down."

"I thought you counted upwards," said Zillah. "You do have some funny ideas here."

"Ten," began Andrew.

"Nine, eight," shouted everyone – everyone except Conrad. He was scowling and still fiddling about with his scum patterns.

By six Zillah was laughing and

joining in the count-down. She spread her arms even wider and waved them up and down wildly.

"Three, two, one – ready –"

SPLASH! They all heard the loud splash. They all saw the water heave and spit. But no one had seen Zillah jump down. Ben watched as the angry water thrashed until it parted and two arms pierced the surface, followed by a terrorized face. But the face didn't belong to Zillah.

"Conrad!" shouted Ben. "It's Conrad. Look, he's in the water!"

Chapter 6

Everything had gone wrong. Alison screamed. Lucy put her hands over her ears, and for Ben time seemed to stop. But somehow he found himself hanging over the outstretched willow branch, looking down into seething splashes. His legs were gripping the bark and scraping painfully as he inched forward.

Conrad was coming up out of the water, but Ben was still too high to reach him. He saw the terror on Conrad's face as the boy's arm reached up and then sank down leaving pulsating flashes of water lacing into one another. He shut his eyes and twisted his body so that his right arm hung even further down. He felt completely cut off from everything except Conrad and the water. He must get him out. He must.

Suddenly there was a terrific weight on his wrist. Conrad had caught hold.

A searing pain jerked his armpit and he knew he couldn't manage to hold Conrad. He remembered Tommy Harris's death. Was this to be the end of him and Conrad? He waited to feel the cold water wrap round him.

But the cold water never came. Instead there was a sudden firmness on his back and he was locked on to the branch, somehow clamped so that he couldn't slip, and the weight was taken from his wrist. Then came the Zillah's reassuring voice, and his fear went. She was on top of him, holding him firm and calling to Conrad.

"Hang on, Conrad. You can do it. Just concentrate. You *will not* drown. The curse has gone. Concentrate on my prism, and I'll soon have you out."

Ben was hardly aware of what happened next, but he was free from

worrying about Conrad. He felt the
weight from his back disappear as
Zillah slid into the water. He was free
to crawl back along the branch and on
to the grass. The next thing he saw
was Conrad shooting up out of the
water like a cork from a bottle, his
arms reaching forwards towards the
bank. Zillah was behind him and out
in a trice.

Ben looked round at everyone in a
dazed way. Lucy still had her hands

over her ears, Andrew had his mouth open and Steven had his fingers in his mouth. Conrad sat there, trembling, with green fronds of slime dripping from his legs and arms and his hair plastered in straight ridges down his forehead. He was wild-eyed. Zillah placed the prism around his neck, then cupped his hands around it. She put an arm round his shoulders.

"You'll calm down if you hold it and watch the colours," she said.

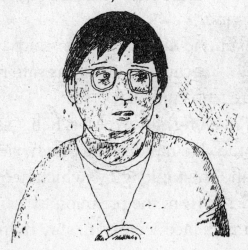

Everyone watched and no one spoke. Ben turned and saw Miss Bell stomping towards them. He felt quite pleased to see her for once. She knelt by Conrad and tried to take charge, but it was Zillah who was in control of everything.

"Don't worry, Miss Bell. He's all right."

"All right!" yelled Miss Bell. "All right, you say! He could have drowned. You all know not to go near the pond."

"Well, he didn't drown," said Zillah, "because the pond is safe now. There's no curse left."

"I'm all right now, Miss Bell," said Conrad. He handed the prism back to Zillah. The pinky glow which had reflected from the prism on to Conrad's face seemed to stay there.

He even managed a smile. He really did look all right. Miss Bell, however, looked very white. She trembled as she made Class Three line up and go straight back to school.

Ben remembered his chocolate. "Have a piece, Miss Bell," he said, tearing down the silver paper and offering her the block. Miss Bell took a

square and thanked him. She began to calm down. Then he gave Conrad and Zillah two pieces each and ate one himself.

Miss Bell took Conrad home, but she was soon back at school, and they had to settle down.

"You were very brave, Zillah," she said, "and so was Ben. You both showed great presence of mind." Ben doodled shyly on his notebook. "Presence of mind": he must remember to ask Mum what that meant.

"It was nothing," said Zillah modestly, "nothing at all, Miss Bell."

Ben didn't hang about after school. He remembered Mrs Turner's weekly and went round straight away with it. She was still sitting watching the world go by when he arrived. Bimbo grabbed the magazine and jumped up on to the table with it. Mrs Turner batted him with a newspaper but it made no difference. Ben laughed. Really, Bimbo could be a naughty dog and Mrs Turner couldn't always control him. Dad would go potty if Bimbo stood on their table.

At bedtime Ben tried his telepathy again. He lay there and tried to concentrate on the caravan and Zillah. He remembered the old lady in the black shawl and wondered if she were still cold. He was surprised when in his mind's eye he saw the old lady. She was holding the Y-shaped hazel twigs. She spoke to Zillah.

"That pond will give them no more trouble now, and my wrongs are put right. We did a good job – or rather *you* did, Zillah."

Ben blinked in the fading twilight. It was almost as if he were dreaming. He shut his eyes and tried to send thoughts to Zillah, but his mind went a blank. It was just as if a screen had come down.

Chapter 7

Ben was out early next morning. The
world had a different feel about it at
half-past eight. It was emptier, sort of
newer feeling. He stood in the middle
of the common, turning round on his
heels and whirling his satchel in the
air, waiting for Steven.

Zillah appeared first. She swung
round the lamp-post, then walked
slowly towards him. "You know,
don't you?" she said. "You know
about the old lady."

Ben remembered last night. He
thought it had been a dream.

Zillah went on. "It wasn't her fault she put a curse on the pond. They were going to burn her. Can you imagine it? They said she was a witch just because she lived on her own and didn't mix much with the villagers. One night, after she'd been burning some bad food, there was a fire and she was blamed. They tied her hands and feet together and threw her into the pond and said if she was a witch, she'd float. If she was not, she'd sink. She sank, but they left her so long down there that she was dead when they got her out."

How horrible. Could it really be true? Ben didn't speak. He didn't know what to say.

Zillah touched his arm. "Don't worry. It all happened a very long time ago. Don't think of the past.

Think of the future." She did a carefree twirl in front of him. "By the way, have you any more of that brown stuff – chocolate? I like your Earth food. We mostly eat energy dust and mineral blocks. It's boring, boring. And I want to walk to school your three-legged way. It sounds crazy. Do you use a hand for a leg or what?"

Ben emptied his pockets and looked idly for string. He was still thinking about the old lady. There was his plastic eye and a half-eaten toffee wrapped in paper but no string.

Zillah pounced on the eye. "I'll swap you this for my long-lasting leaf," she said. Ben hesitated. The eye was rather special. Uncle Bob had got it from work, where they printed false eyes. The leaf looked even more

special, though. It still looked fresh.

"All right," he said and they
exchanged their treasures.

"If it sprouts, give Lucy a piece,"
said Zillah.

Andrew and Steven came running
up. They were acting the fool as usual.
Andrew had his fingertips against his
forehead. "Don't interrupt my
telepathy," he joked. "I hear quacking
noises from the pond. They're going
'quack, quack, quack'." Zillah pushed
him and he went quacking round in
circles.

"There will be ducks here one day," she said. "You wait and see. Now, don't turn round. Just concentrate and guess who is coming up behind you. He's wearing yellow."

"The man in the moon," said Andrew.

"Conrad," said Steven. "I expect his school shirt's still drying."

"See, it's working," said Zillah.

Conrad joined them. "Hello," he said, then paused and scratched his cheek. "I'm . . . sorry about yesterday. You must think me a proper twit, falling in and spoiling things."

Steven slapped him on the back as acceptance of the apology.

"Thanks, Zillah," said Conrad. "I don't know what I would have done without you. Thanks especially as . . ." He didn't get a chance to finish.

"You'd have got out anyway," interrupted Zillah, "but I knew you were frightened. There really is no curse left, you know." Conrad bit his lips and smiled weakly.

"It must have worked or you'd have drowned," said Ben. He shuddered. "Old Ding-dong gave us a right rocket about going there, though."

"I bet," said Conrad. "I feel differently about the pond now. Let's go over and see if it looks different." They ran across the grass.

"It's still dull and lifeless," said Steven. But almost as soon as he'd spoken, a shaft of morning sunlight shot through the trees and parted the water by a stone. Something jumped off the stone and swam away, then something jumped off another stone, and the water swirled into rings.

"Frogs," said Ben.

"It's not lifeless after all," said Andrew. Another frog jumped in, and another, and another. "Look, they're everywhere. Not quite as good as ducks, but it's a start. Come on, we'd better get going. Race you to school."

Chapter 8

Ben worked hard and finished his sums quickly, then he looked out of the window at his special tree. It was as beautiful as ever.

"Ben Jarvis," called Miss Bell, "are you dreaming again?" Dreaming, the very idea. No, he was concentrating, not dreaming. He was concentrating on what the school would look like from the topmost branch of his special tree, but he couldn't tell her that. Instead he took up his maths book to be marked. Miss Bell ticked every single sum and smiled.

"Well done, Ben Jarvis," she said. "Just look what you can do when you concentrate." Ben felt pleased. He had concentrated on his sums and it had worked, like the telepathy had. It seemed good stuff, this concentration. Perhaps he'd do it more often.

Things went very well in Class Three until Andrew upset a pot of blue paint in the afternoon. Then it all altered. Some paint trickled into the guinea pigs' cage, and poor Thumper

got a blue nose. Miss Bell had to take him out to be cleaned and Andrew was told to mop up the paint.

As soon as Miss Bell and Thumper had left the room Jonathan Turvey stood up and spoke.

"What's all this about Zillah saving Conrad?" he asked. They told him all about the special ceremony and Conrad's accident in high, babbling voices.

"Rubbish!" said Jonathan. "Don't believe it."

"It's true," chorused the class.

"Well, how did she do it? How did she save Conrad?"

"I communicated properly, that's all," said Zillah.

"'I communicated properly, that's all'," mimicked Jonathan in a sing-songy voice. "You sound like some posho. You're weird. You say odd things. I think you used some sort of magic. You're like a sorcerer."

"Sit down, Turvey!" yelled Steven. "No one asked you what you thought."

Suddenly Lucy got up. She shouted out and surprised them all. "It's a

good job Zillah was there. She's kind and brave, that's what – and clever," she added, "so shut just up, Jonathan Turvey." She sat down and wriggled her back against the chair as if shrinking back to size, but her face still held its determined look.

"I bet it's that prism she wears," went on Jonathan Turvey. "It's a charm thing with special powers. Goodness knows what else she can do with it. It might be something evil next time."

Zillah dragged it roughly over her head. She threw it at him. "There," she said. "You wear it and see what you can do, then." It flashed through the spectrum of colours as he put it on until it settled, clear and heavy, on his grey shirt.

"Come on, Turvey," said Conrad. "Let's see what you can do. Do something really fantastic, go on." Jonathan shut his eyes. He screwed them up tight but nothing happened.

"Go on," said Allison. "We're waiting. If you can't do anything, give it back." She stood up, her pointed chin thrust forward.

"No," shouted Jonathan. "You're not having it. You . . ."

But Alison was across the room before he could finish. She made a grab for it. Jonathan spun it round his neck till it hung down his back, then he leaned against the chair and trapped it there.

Ben heard footsteps. "Miss Bell!" he yelled. Everyone sat down quickly except Jonathan and Alison.

Miss Bell slammed the door shut

90

and looked grim. She put Thumper back in his cage, then turned to the class. "I'm waiting, Class Three, for an explanation of all the noise." No one spoke for a second, then gradually the story came out and Miss Bell got really cross. She walked up and down the classroom tutting and grumbling. In the end she made them clear away the paints.

When they were all sitting down again Miss Bell collected their pictures. As she passed Jonathan Turvey she ordered him to give the prism back to Zillah immediately. He stood up, took it off, turned, then stopped. Miss Bell looked to the back of the classroom. At Zillah's desk there was just an empty chair.

She walked over. On the table were eight pieces of torn painting. Miss Bell moved them around. They fitted together like a jigsaw puzzle to form a misty moon circled by six planets. At the edge of the picture was a ghostly image of a tall figure in a stripy jumper disappearing into a cluster of jewel-like stars. Its arm was raised in a farewell wave.

Chapter 9

Zillah was not at school next day. Miss Bell asked if anyone had seen her. No one had. They'd searched the village for her. Ben had asked Mrs Turner, and Conrad had done the bravest thing of all. He'd been back to the gypsy site all on his own. The caravan was completely empty.

Miss Bell marked Zillah absent and shut the register. "Now line up ready for assembly, Class Three, then go quickly and quietly into the hall."

Class Three went quickly but they were not quiet until they reached the hall, when a sudden silence sliced through them.

Mr Spriggott was standing in the middle of the hall. He had his back to them and his arms folded firmly in front of him. He did not even turn round when Class Three arrived. He was staring up at the wall, gently moving his head from side to side.

He was looking at a painting. it was

a painting of a village pond. The pond was at the edge of a common, and behind it peeped a church. At the other side, further down the road, was a school. The picture was framed with tiny flowers. Insects with gossamer wings hung in a beam of sunshine, which was so delicate that it seemed to shimmer. A twisty willow tree overhung the pond, and on the water, with feathers which glistened, were two ducks and five little ducklings. Underneath, in large gold letters were the words "'MIDDLE HILL VILLAGE POND' WITH LOVE FROM ZILLAH. EARTH, 20TH CENTURY".

No one spoke. They just gasped. Ben fingered the square leaf in his pocket. Would it sprout, or would it die?

"My word!" said Miss Bell at last, then because she couldn't think of anything else to say she said it again. "My word!"

Ben watched her slowly pat the bun at the back of her head, then turn and gaze out of the window. He followed her gaze. Cheek – she was staring at his special tree shining gold against the blue sky. Don't say Miss Bell had started dreaming too!